WILD DEVOTION

WILD HEART MOUNTAIN: WILD RIDERS MC
BOOK THIRTEEN

SADIE KING

WILD RIDERS MC

AN INTRODUCTION

Welcome to Wild Heart Mountain home of the Wild Riders MC.

If you love damaged heroes and curvy girl romance, then you'll love the Wild Riders MC.

This group of ex-military bikers fall hard and fall fast when they encounter the curvy women who heal their hearts.

Expect forbidden love, age gap, forced proximity, fake relationships, single dads, single moms and off-limits love with protective heroes who will do anything for the women they love.

Spend some time with Wild Heart Mountain's Wild Riders MC, the MC that's all heart.

Let me introduce you to the members…

Ex-military buddies **Raiden, Quentin and Travis** formed the Wild Riders MC when they got out of the military and wanted to create a place for veterans who love to ride.

They set up their headquarters in a compound on the side of Wild Heart Mountain.

Travis, whose road name is Hops, runs the Wild Taste Bar and Restaurant, and secretly crushes on his best friend's sister.

Quentin, also known as Barrels, runs the award-winning Wild Taste Brewery located out the back of the restaurant. He was a First Class Sargent in the army and you wouldn't want to cross him. Especially where his little sister is concerned…

Colter, or Vintage, is a motorbike mechanic and runs the bike shop. He collects old bikes and loves all things vintage, especially the bubbly Danni and her 1950s curves.

Calvin, also known as Badge, is the local Sheriff and his uptight views are shaped by loss.

Joseph, or Lone Star, is a recluse whose military experiences have given him a distaste for humanity.

Grant goes by Snips. He's the local barber and recently

discovered he has a child. He's learning to navigate life as a single dad.

Arlo earns the road name Prince because of his charming and personable nature. He loves getting under the skin of Maggie, the shy pastry chef.

Davis begins the series as a prospect. Younger than most of the other men, he came out of the military with diminished hearing. His hearing aids make him shy with women and he keeps himself hidden away.

Specs would rather read a book than talk to anyone.

Bit Rate is a grumpy single dad widower in need of a nanny.

Judge is a military lawyer and always does the right thing, until he meets the curvy woman who makes him question his world view.

Luke becomes a prospect after Raiden finds him drinking himself to oblivion in a strip joint. A wheelchair user since he lost both his legs in Afghanistan, Luke finds new purpose with the MC, but can he find love?

Marcus goes by Wood because his family owns the local sawmill and it's his medium of choice. He channels his PTSD into his art, creating sculptures that attract the attention of an arts journalist from the city.

On the other side of Wild Heart Mountain is a town called Hope, with the Emerald Heart Resort nestled in the nearby hills. During the summer, it's a popular destination for tourists and in winter, they come for the ski season. Perfect for a snowed in romance…

Stay awhile in Wild Heart Mountain and explore the other series set here.

Wild Heart Mountain: Military Heroes
Wild Heart Mountain: Mountain Heroes
Temptation
A Runaway Bride for Christmas
A Secret Baby for Christmas

WILD DEVOTION

WILD RIDERS MC

A wounded warrior and the single mom he'll do anything to protect.

I came back from Afghanistan a broken man, missing two limbs and resigned to life in a wheelchair.

The Wild Riders MC brought me back from the brink of darkness.

I've accepted my new way of life until I meet Isla.

She's on the run with a newborn baby, exhausted and in need of refuge.

Isla awakens something long dormant in me. She reminds me what it means to serve and protect.

I'll do anything to keep Isla and the baby safe, even if she'll only ever see me as half a man.

But when her past catches up with her, can I be the man she needs?

Wild Devotion is a steamy instalove romance featuring an ex-military wounded hero and the curvy single mom who awakens his protective instincts.

www.authorsadieking.com

WILD DEVOTION

.

1

LUKE

a slow burn courses through the pectoral muscles in my chest as I pull the bar towards me. The strain is almost too much, and I grunt as my muscles fatigue and threaten to give up.

"Come on, Luke, one more." Arlo hovers over the bench with his hands under the bar, ready to catch the weights if my muscles give up.

But I'm not giving up. I push through the strain and raise the bar one last time, letting out a grunt as every muscle in my upper body screams.

"Nice one." Arlo grabs the bar and helps me hook it back into place.

I lie on the bench panting as my muscles ease back to their normal state. I'll be sore tomorrow, but a good sore. The kind that means I'm getting stronger.

Arlo chucks my gym towel at me and offers a hand. I grip his hand, and he pulls me up to a sitting position. My useless limbs stick out under my gym shorts. But with just the two of us here, I don't bother to hide the stumps where my legs used to be.

Arlo checks his phone for the hundredth time since we started the workout.

"Still no word from Maggie?" I ask.

"Not since she picked Isla up at the station." He runs a hand over his beard and a frown line creases his brow.

He glances out the one grimy window of the basement gym. It's up high and shows the snow-covered parking lot.

"I should have gone with her," he says for about the hundredth time.

It's no use telling him what he already knows, that Maggie snuck out of the kitchen without telling Arlo because she wanted to go alone. Without knowing the situation of the woman she was meeting, I'm guessing she didn't want her big hairy biker husband scaring her off.

"Maybe they needed to get supplies for the baby. They might have gone shopping in Hope."

Arlo grunts but doesn't seem convinced. "We've got plenty of baby stuff here. The damn club's turning into a nursery."

He's not wrong. Since I joined the MC as a prospect two years ago, I've been to six weddings, I've lost count of the number of babies born, and at least two of the old ladies are pregnant right now.

There's a pang in my chest so strong that I close my eyes.

Marriage and babies, a family. My young self never

thought of those things when I signed up for the military at eighteen. Having a family was the last thing on my mind. I wanted adventure and to follow family tradition. My dad served and my grandad served. Joining the army was all I ever wanted to do.

Now at twenty-seven, I sense the loss of all the things I'll never have.

The pang of loss goes through my body, and a violent itch makes my missing left leg twitch. The stump thumps against the bench and I grit my teeth, waiting for the phantom itch to dissipate.

Arlo notes my discomfort, but he knows better than to say anything. The last thing I want is pity from the men.

"Do we know the woman's situation?" I ask, trying to distract my brain from the itch that isn't there.

"She left her fiancé." Arlo paces to the window and back, frowning at the snow falling against the windowpane.

It must be a shitty situation for a woman to take her baby and leave her fiancé on Christmas Eve. We've got a woman's refuge in the mountains that Lone Star's old lady set up. It saddens me how much it's needed.

"Maggie was at culinary school with Isla's brother. I've met him a few times. He does the competition circuit as well." Arlo's referring to the pastry competitions Maggie loves taking part in.

"Can't the brother take her in?"

Arlo shakes his head. "He's away in Europe and his wife is having complications with her pregnancy, so she can't fly and he doesn't want to leave her. He gave Isla Maggie's number."

Arlo glances out the snow-covered window again. "They should be back by now."

What he needs is a distraction until Maggie gets back safely.

"Your turn." My wheelchair is parked next to the bench, and I pull it towards me. I slide into the chair and wheel around behind the bench, ready to spot Arlo.

We're working out in the basement gym at the Wild Riders MC headquarters. Even though it's Christmas Eve, I don't miss a workout. My legs might be useless, but my upper body, core, and arms are strong.

Arlo does three sets and Maggie still isn't back. He paces the gym while I haul myself back onto the bench and get ready for sit-ups.

Arlo hovers, but he knows better than to hold my limbs down. I hate anyone touching my stumps, but when I first started working out, my body had gotten soft from no use. I avoided core exercises until I finally gave in and let Arlo strap my stumps down while I curled up to a sitting position.

Now my core is strong, but I still need straps to counterbalance the weight. I secure them loosely around my upper thighs.

We've been working out for an hour, and despite the snow outside, sweat runs over my body.

I pull my t-shirt off and place it behind my head. My goal is to get to 100 sit-ups by the end of the year, and I'm eight days away.

I get into a steady rhythm, breathing in on the up and out on the back down. Sweat glistens on my stomach, and I focus on the rhythm of my breathing as I count up in my head.

Without my lower legs to counterbalance, my abs and upper legs are working extra hard. When I started working out two years ago, I could barely do five assisted sit-ups.

My physical therapist told me getting to ten unassisted would be good. I'm not looking for good. My lower body might be missing, but my torso and arms can be strong.

The sensation of my muscles straining spurs me on as I hit the halfway mark.

I'm in the zone now, my muscles working extra hard to pull myself up. I pass sixty, then seventy, then eighty.

Every muscle in my stomach, back, and upper legs screams and sweat flies off my forehead, but I remain laser focused on pulling myself up one sit-up at a time.

I reach ninety and my body shudders. I'm vaguely aware of Arlo moving across the room and voices at the door.

But I remain focused on pushing past ninety. My body strains and my muscles burn. I cry out with every sit-up.

Shapes move in my peripheral vision, and a baby wails.

I'm at ninety-five, and my lungs are it fit to burst. My body gives out and my abdominals freeze up. The next time I come down, my body refuses to get back up.

I lie back on the bench, breathing hard. Ninety-five. That's five more than last time, but still not the hundred sit-ups I promised myself I'd get to by the end of the year.

As I lie panting on my back, the rest of the basement comes back into focus. Maggie's voice reaches my ears, along with the sound of a baby crying.

My abs are protesting, but I grip the side of the bench and pull myself up one last time. I'm panting hard as I sit up on the bench. My chest heaves up and down, and my hair sticks to my forehead.

I'm a sweaty mess with no shirt on and my stumps sticking out of my gym shorts. But it's only Maggie and she's practically family. But it's not only Maggie.

Learning on the doorframe with a baby clutched to her chest is the prettiest woman I'm ever seen. Her dark hair falls over her face as she comforts the child with shushing noises. She jiggles it up and down, making her entire curvy body move in a way that shouldn't be sexy. But it is.

My dick stirs to life, which is a surprise. I've not felt that for a real live woman since the accident.

My heart, already hammering in my chest, picks up a notch and threatens to burst right out of my rib cage.

Arlo's saying something, but I don't hear what it is. All my focus is on the goddess in front of me.

"The refuge is full, so Isla will be staying at the club," Arlo says.

My thoughts are all jumbled up and I open my mouth

to speak, but the only sound that comes out is a gargled, "Aha."

The woman glances up and our eyes lock. She has dark circles under hers, and they appear haunted. If some fucker has harmed her, I'll track him down and, missing limbs or not, I'll fucking hurt him.

Her gaze rakes over my chest, and her eyes widen when she gets to the six-pack of my abs. My dick stirs again, and a sensation long forgotten flutters through my veins.

Attraction.

This is what it's like to be mutually attracted to some-one. I puff out my chest, aware of my well-defined muscles, especially with the badass tattoo that curves around my bulging biceps.

Then her eyes track further down my body.

Panic grips my insides, and I flick my gym towel over my stumps. I look away before her gaze gets to my useless stumps sticking out of my gym shorts. Before she realizes that I'm only half a man.

I can't handle seeing the pity in this woman's eyes. For a moment I forgot. For a moment, I was just a hard-muscled man enjoying the appreciative gaze of a pretty woman.

Pressing my knuckles into the bench, I breathe deeply, not looking up until Arlo and Maggie and the girl holding the baby have left.

Their voices fade as they head down the corridor and to the stairs, not giving it a second thought as they climb the stairs with their working limbs.

I wait for a long time until my breathing has calmed, and the sweat has turned icy on my body. Only then do I haul myself into my wheelchair and maneuver around the gym equipment, squeeze through the door, and wheel down the corridor that's so tight my elbows bump the walls as I roll by until I get to the elevator.

2

ISLA

*C*ody's entire face puckers up, and his cheeks go red.

"Oh no you don't." I pull him to my chest and jiggle him up and down in a way that's supposed to be soothing, but it's too late. An almighty wail erupts out of his tiny mouth, which seems too small to be making such a big noise.

I slide off the bed and pace the room, whispering lullabies into the top of his downy head. But Cody keeps on crying.

"Are you hungry?" I fed him ten minutes ago, but I unlatch my nursing bra and offer him my breast. He turns his head away and cries louder.

"Do you need changing?" I only just changed his diaper, but I lay him on the bed to check again. But when I touch the diaper, my hand comes away dry.

"What is it, sweet pea?" I hold him out in front of me

with my arms straight so his crying face is level with mine. "I don't know what you need."

Cody squeezes his eyes shut and cries louder.

"I know how you feel, buddy." Twenty-four hours ago, we were in a warm apartment in Charlotte with all his cuddly toys and familiar blankets.

Now we're in a room at the top of a motorcycle club headquarters where burly men prowl the corridors and the only familiar face is a friend of my brother's who he knows from culinary school.

Yesterday I was the fiancé of an investment banker, a new mother taking maternity leave from her marketing job, living in a penthouse apartment in the swanky part of town and planning the perfect society wedding. Today I'm a runaway, a single mom with no home address and no plan for the future.

A shiver runs down my spine. Whenever I think about the future, all I see in my mind is a black hole. I have no idea what my life will look like now. I can't go back to my job, not when the man I just left was the CEO's son. I don't have a place to live. It was Ian's apartment. My family probably isn't going to speak to me for canceling the 'wedding of the season' as Ian's mom keeps calling it on social media. Mom won't forgive me for giving up the 'perfect' life and relegating her grandchild to life with a single parent.

But as I stare into the crumpled face of my unhappy son, conviction settles in my chest. "I've done the right thing."

If I say it out loud, my brain might start to believe it.

I take a few deep breaths, trying to calm myself. "I'm safe," I say with every out breath. "I'm safe. I'm safe. I'm safe."

More at peace, I fold Cody into my chest. "We're safe, sweet pea." I kiss the top of his head and repeat the refrain until he stops crying.

"I know this all feels different, but Mommy's here and we're going to be okay."

The words are as much to reassure me as they are to reassure him. He must feel the tension and unease that I've been carrying for the last forty-eight hours, ever since I made the decision to leave.

"We're going to be okay."

There's a gentle knock on the door, and when I open it Maggie is there with a Christmas hat sitting askew on her chestnut hair.

"You ready to come down and meet the family?" She smiles kindly, and a well of emotion threatens to overspill.

I only met Maggie once when my brother Ryan graduated, but when I called my brother and told him I was in trouble, he put me in touch with Maggie.

Ryan is away in Italy, and his wife Julia is having complications with her pregnancy. I hated putting him on the spot like that. He implored me to call Mom, but I can't. She's been planning mine and Ian's wedding since we were in kindergarten.

To her, our relationship is perfect, and on the outside, it looks that way. At first it was, but slowly over time Ian turned into someone quite different. It happened slowly.

A harsh word there, a derogatory comment there, until it turned into daily criticism of everything I do. His tempers are swift and harsh, and I found myself creeping around the house, not wanting to say anything to upset him.

In the office he was different, charming and well-liked, but at home I saw the real Ian, the one I couldn't tell anyone about. The mood swings, the temper, and the fear always bubbling under the surface that he could turn violent.

He's the golden boy, the son of my parent's best friends. The up and coming young millionaire set to take over the family business before he's thirty.

On paper he's a catch. Behind closed doors, he's a mean psychological bully who's worn away my self-esteem over the three years we've been dating.

I thought things would improve once the baby came along, but they got worse. His angry outbursts got more erratic and the hint of violence more present.

Two days ago, during an argument over nothing more than what the party favors should be at the wedding, he threw his drink at me. The glass hit the wall just behind my head. I'm not sure if he aimed to miss or if he meant to hit me with it. I was nursing Cody at the time and the tumbler shattered, sending sharp shards of glass over both of us.

I thought I could live with a man who got angry sometimes, but picking shards of glass out of the hair of my four-week-old baby was the wake up call I needed.

Ian walked out, and I called Ryan and finally came

clean about the monster I've been living with. He made some calls and hooked me up with Maggie. Her husband is part of the Wild Riders motorcycle club, and they run a women's refuge in the mountains.

Only it's full, since apparently Ian isn't the only one who turns into a mega asshole at this time of year. So here I am on Christmas Day, staying in one of the spare rooms of a motorcycle club. Out of the frying pan and into the fire.

But the people I've met here so far seem nice. Arlo, Maggie's husband, called around, and by the time I arrived there was a bassinet, diapers, baby toys, and clothing waiting for me.

Someone made up a bed in a spare room, and I fell into a fitful sleep late last night with Cody waking up every few hours fussing at the unfamiliar surroundings.

I want to stay in this room and hide, but I need to say thank you to the women who pooled together to get me the things I need.

I take a deep breath and give Maggie a shaky smile. "I'll come down."

Maggie puts a hand on my shoulder. "You're safe here, Isla, and everyone is friendly. You're under the protection of the club now."

Under the protection of the club. Her words make me shiver. I don't know these men; I don't know what they're into. But Ryan wouldn't have sent me here if it wasn't safe.

"Come on." Maggie hustles me toward the door and I follow.

. . .

A few hours later, I'm seated at the long table that is made up of smaller tables pushed together. The meal was excellent, the most I've eaten for days, and I'm drowsy.

I barely spoke to anyone all night. I've kept my focus on Cody and making sure he has what he needs. There are a lot of kids here. It's more family oriented than I thought an MC would be. The women are kind and the men are terrifying. Lots of beards and tattoos, although some of them are clean-shaven and very much the ex-military men that Maggie's explained they all are. A motorcycle club full of veterans. No wonder Ryan thought I'd be safe here.

Across the table from me sits the man in the wheel-chair who was in the gym when I first arrived. I try not to look at him as I feed Cody.

When I arrived yesterday, exhausted from the train, he was a sight for sore eyes, that's for sure. His muscular body was sweaty with exertion as he pushed himself to the limit.

I long to ask him what happened to his legs, but it wouldn't be polite. Besides, he's not spoken to me, not like some of the other men who have politely asked about the baby. They're new fathers, proud to tell me about their own little ones and offer advice on why Cody might be crying so much.

I know why he's crying so much. Because he senses his mother's unease.

I've kept my head down, and they probably think it's

because I'm furtive and scared, but it's not. I'm so damn embarrassed to be in this situation.

I grew up with all the advantages of life: two parents with good jobs, a beautiful home in a nice neighborhood, in a wealthy country. I have a college education and a professional job. I've had every advantage; I should be kicking it at life. And yet, I still ended up here, a single mom on the run with no idea what her future holds.

If I told the carefree Isla of a few years ago that she'd be spending Christmas with her baby in a refuge after escaping an emotionally abusive relationship, I wouldn't have believed myself. I'm so embarrassed I can't look anyone in the eye.

Cody gives a yawn, and it sets me off. I haven't been sleeping well with all the feeding and attention he needs and then the excitement of the last few days. It's early, but I long to be upstairs on our own.

I stand up and catch Maggie's eye. "I'm going up to bed."

I've already been told they won't let me help with the clearing up. There's a lot of fuss made over new mothers here, and I'm grateful. I can concentrate on caring for my baby and getting him what he needs. Right now, what he needs is for both of us to get some sleep.

I hold Cody close and cross the room.

"Isla." I turn at my name to find the man in the wheelchair holding out one of my muslin cloths. He's got deep blue eyes that remind me of the ocean where we used to vacation as children. "You dropped this."

"Thank you." I take the cloth and he holds onto it a

17

little too long, so when I pull it out of his hands, he doesn't drop it.

"You're safe here." His voice is gravelly, deeper than someone his age should sound. I guess he's a few years older than me, but there are lines around his eyes like he's been through more than a man in his twenties should. "I'll personally make sure of that."

His gaze is determined, and I'm reassured by his look. I'm reminded of his hard torso glistening with sweat that I glimpsed at the gym, and heat creeps up my neck.

"How did you know my name?" We weren't introduced at the gym, and he hasn't spoken to me all evening.

He smiles, and in that smile I see the shadow of a carefree boy, perhaps the young man he used to be before whatever horrendous thing happened to his limbs. "I made it my job to know. If I'm providing protection for you and Cody, I had to know your names."

He glances at Cody, and his expression softens. "If there's anything you need, anything at all, let me know."

Protection. The word warms my chest. I've spent the last few months with a growing sense of uneasiness. And for the first time in as long as I can remember, I feel truly safe.

"Thank you."

He drops his hold on the muslin cloth, and I tuck it into my arms under Cody.

"Goodnight," he whispers as I turn away.

3

LUKE

The sound of a door unlatching has me jerking awake. It's still dark outside, and the chill pre-dawn air chases away any last vestiges of sleep.

The door to Isla's room pushes open, and Isla steps into the corridor. She carries Cody wrapped in a sling around her chest, and a large coat covers the both of them. A woolen beanie is pulled over her hair, leaving the ends sticking out at all angles. She looks fucking adorable.

Isla stops when she sees me, and her mouth drops open in surprise. She takes in my wheelchair and the blanket that's fallen from around my shoulders. Her eyes narrow in suspicion. "Did you sleep out here?"

When I said I'd provide protection, I wasn't joking. I may be in a wheelchair, but I'm still a military man at my core. A woman needs protection, and I'll do whatever I can to provide that.

"I said I'd keep you safe."

She blinks quickly and looks away, and I hope she doesn't think sleeping outside her door is creepy. That's the last thing I want.

I put on my best smile, and it turns into a yawn. "Is it even morning yet?"

I run a hand over my face, and it catches on stubble. I'm stiff from spending the night in my chair and I need a shower, but it's worth it to be here to see Isla and Cody.

"It's almost six-thirty, but he's been up since five."

The dark smudges under her eyes are even more pronounced since yesterday. "I'm taking him for a walk. It usually helps settle him."

There's no way I'm letting Isla wander around on her own when it's still dark outside.

"I'll join you."

She looks at me in surprise but doesn't protest as I follow her down the hall. I stop at the elevator, and she continues down the stairs. "I'll see you down there."

It's an agonizing wait for the elevator, and I hope like hell she doesn't try to leave without me. It's a relief when I reach the ground floor and Isla's waiting for me.

"You don't have to do this. I'm sure you've got better things to do with your day than babysit."

Her brow creases in a little frown, like she's trying to figure out why I'm here. It saddens me that she's suspicious of a guy wanting to help out.

"You're doing the babysitting. I'm just making sure you're okay."

She follows me to the back door, and I stop by the coat rack. She tilts her head, her eyes narrowing, still not believing I'm here because I want to be here. Or maybe she's wondering if I'm not capable of looking after her because I'm in a wheelchair.

"Has the club ordered you to watch me? That's how this works, isn't it?"

I grab my coat and shrug it over my shoulders. My gloves are in my pocket and I slip those on too, then check that Isla's got gloves. Cody snuggles against her chest with a knitted hat covering his tiny head. "Is he going to be warm enough out there?"

I've been around enough babies at the clubhouse to know they get cold pretty quick, especially newborns.

Isla buttons up her coat so it covers the both of them, and his little head peeks out the top. She smiles warmly at him. "He's got my body heat, and we won't stay out for long."

Satisfied they're both ready for the cold, I push open the door and answer Isla's question.

"I volunteered."

What I don't mention is that I didn't give anyone else the opportunity to say otherwise.

I told Raiden I would spend the night here and move my stuff in tomorrow. As long as Isla and Cody are here, I'm here.

It's stopped snowing, and the thin layer covering the ground crunches under my wheels. It's crispy but not yet slippery.

I'm limited to where I can go around here while in my wheelchair. Raiden had the entire compound re-concreted, so it's easy for me to get around without bumping up against uneven surfaces. Man, I owe that guy a lot.

There are some mountain trails that have boardwalks and well-tended even paths, but others are bumpy with tree roots and rocks and mud, especially with the snow we've had.

I've got a set of prosthetics, but I hate wearing them, and I don't want to draw attention to my missing limbs by stopping to put them on. I hope a few laps of the compound is enough to give Cody whatever it is he needs to get to sleep.

Isla falls into step beside me. "I don't think Ian's going to come looking for me."

At mention of her ex, my hands clench into fists. I don't know what the asshole did, but it was enough to make her run on Christmas Eve. He doesn't deserve Isla or Cody. "What makes you say that?"

She takes a moment to answer. "I think it will be a relief to him that I'm gone."

I huff out a big breath. If Isla and Cody were mine, I'd search to the ends of the Earth to find them.

"Then he's a fool."

We round the side of the building, and the valley comes into view with the first dawn light tingeing the sky gray. There's a narrow path that runs around to the front of the restaurant, and I drop back so we can go single file.

Isla waits for me at the front of the restaurant, staring out at the valley. I wheel up next to her, and we say nothing for a long while as the sky turns from gray to pink.

"I'm scared." She says it so quietly I almost miss it.

My hand reaches for hers, and I curl her fingers into mine. Even through our gloves, I feel the spark of warmth that radiates from her. I have no right to hold her hand, but she doesn't pull away.

"I won't let him hurt you again."

She shakes her head. "He never hurt me, not physically." She shivers, and I tighten my grip on her fingers. "Not yet."

Her voice wobbles, and she presses her lips together. She looks scared for a moment until she swallows it down. Her hand comes up to the Cody-shaped lump in her coat, and she rubs his back in slow circles. I wonder if she's soothing him or herself.

A fierce protectiveness flashes through me, and with it an agonizing frustration at my limitations.

I wish I could be the man she needs; I wish I could stand up and take her in my arms and tell her it will all be okay.

If I was a whole man, I'd hunt the fucker down and make him pay for the fear he's put into Isla. But all I can offer is protection while she's here. While she's in my clubhouse, where I have an adapted space, I can move freely in and my MC brothers to stand by me.

"I'm scared of what comes next," she whispers. "I ran to get away from Ian, but I don't know what I'm running to."

I squeeze her hand. I can already tell from the short

time I've known Isla that she's a smart woman. "You'll figure it out."

Cody gurgles, and she glances down at him and smiles. "He's asleep, at last."

Relief sags her shoulders, and she sways on her feet. I put out a steadying hand. "Are you sleeping?"

She sighs. "Sometimes. But not enough."

The answer doesn't fill me with confidence. I spent a lot of time last night online learning everything I could about newborn babies, and it was chilling. It seems all they do is eat and poop and take short naps and cry for no reason. They literally drain their mothers who don't get enough sleep and forget to eat.

The thought occurs to me that Isla's been awake for hours and probably had nothing to eat. "Are you eating?"

"I had a good meal yesterday."

She's not sleeping, and there's no one to help with the baby. I thought protection was what Isla needs, but that's only half the story. She needs sleep, and food, and help with the baby.

It's Boxing Day, but I'm calling in an emergency club meeting.

But first of all, Isla's getting a decent meal. "We're going inside, and I'm making you a big breakfast."

She shakes her head. "I can't. You've already done so much."

I nudge her with my elbow, and she starts walking. "I don't want to hear that again. You're here as our guest, and I'm looking after you."

She gives me a grateful look as we head inside.

. . .

Two hours later, I've cooked Isla eggs and bacon for breakfast. Danni is watching Cody, so Isla can take a shower and a nap.

I've called an emergency meeting, and now I face the grumpy faces of my MC brothers across the meeting room table.

"This better be good, Chariot. I'm hungover, and I haven't had breakfast yet," mumbles Snips.

Right on cue, Maggie bursts into the meeting room carrying a tray of crispy bacon. The smell wafts through the room, making the men sit up.

She's followed by her son Benji, proudly brandishing two loaves of bread with a huge grin on his toddler face. Bettie, Danni's oldest, carries the ketchup, holding it carefully in her chubby fingers.

"Bacon sandwiches to sweeten the sting."

I swallow hard, hoping I've read my brothers right and they're not about to turn on me and chuck me out of the club. I only got patched in a few months ago, and this is the first favor I've asked.

Still, calling a club meeting at nine a.m. on Boxing Day is a pretty bold move.

Maggie puts the tray in the middle of the table and the men attack the food eagerly.

I swallow nervously and glance at Raiden. The Prez has his arms folded and eyes me like my old Sergeant Major used to.

He agreed to call the meeting for me, but I'm aware of

the risk he's taking. He's also away from his family, and his old lady doesn't put up with any shit. I promised a week of babysitting duties if he'd hear me out.

I wait until everyone has a bacon sandwich and Maggie has herded the kids out of the room.

"Isla needs our help."

Judge frowns and swallows a mouthful of sandwich. "Is that the woman with the baby who's staying upstairs?"

"Yeah."

"Seems we're already giving her help," grumbles Snips. He looks particularly rough this morning, and I'm reminded of the bottle of whiskey he insisted on finishing late last night.

"We've given her club protection," Raiden says.

All eyes turn to Prez. He remains leaning against the wall, but the steely tone of his voice is a reminder to everyone what club protection means.

If the club offers anyone protection, then we protect them with our lives. We're all veterans here. We all know what that means.

"Her ex might turn up, and he could be dangerous," I state. "She claims he was never violent towards her, but a desperate man might do anything."

There are nods all round.

"I'm moving in while she's here," I state. "I'll be the main guard."

Snips swallows his sandwich and lets out a belch. "Excuse me," he mutters.

Barrels shifts in his seat and fixes me with a steely stare. "No offense Luke, you're one tough motherfucker,

26

no doubt about that, but do you think you're the best man for this job?"

A spike of hurt pierces my chest at the implication that I might not be capable of protecting a woman. But Barrels almost made it to Sergeant Major before leaving the military. He doesn't say it to be hurtful. He says it because he's thinking of what's best for the mission.

My hands clench into fists, and I push them against the arms of my chair so I rise up on my fists. Perhaps he's right. Maybe a cripple isn't the right choice to protect a woman. But I can guarantee no man here feels the way I do about Isla. What I lack in body parts I make up for in determination. There is no way I'd let anyone get to Isla.

"Let him try me." I grit out the words, and the room falls silent. Several sets of eyes stare at me in surprise.

Then Bit Rate chuckles. "You've got it bad, man."

I turn my head, and the smile slides off his face. "I've got a woman and baby who are running scared. Let that fucker come near her, and I'll show him what a cripple can do."

It's big talk, and I hope like hell I can follow through. But there's no way in hell I'm leaving this up to anyone else.

Snips clears his throat. "If you're intent on being this woman's superhero, why the hell are we all here?"

Good point. I take a calming breath and get onto the real reason I called the meeting.

"Isla doesn't just need protection; she's struggling with a newborn baby. She's up all night feeding, she's not sleeping enough, that's making her more anxious, and that makes the baby anxious, and then the baby doesn't want to sleep and she sleeps even less."

"You want us to look after her baby?" Specs looks incredulous, and I don't blame him. He's the only man left, apart from me, who's still flying the single flag.

"No. I want your old ladies to."

The guys look at each other, finally getting it.

"She needs round the clock help. She needs meals cooked for her. She needs someone to watch the baby so she can shower and get some time to herself, and she needs someone to do pick up a night feed so she can keep sleeping. Does anyone have one of those breast pump expressing thingies?" I hold my hand up and squeeze my fingers together in an attempt to mimic an expressing machine.

There are some raised eyebrows, but I'm not going to explain the hours I've spent on the internet learning about breastfeeding and expressing and chaffing and all this other shit I never knew I needed to know about keeping a baby alive.

Some of the men looked blank, since not all the ladies choose to breastfeed, but Hops pipes up.

"Yeah, we've got one that's still works. You'll need bags to store the milk, and new bottle nipples."

"We've got some spare breast milk bags," chimes in Barrels, which I'm pretty sure is a line the ex-First Class Sergeant never thought he'd ever say back in his military days.

The rest of the meeting turns into a discussion on what their old ladies have and what we need to buy and the best way to store breast milk. Phone calls are made to the women, and pretty soon we've got a roster worked out, I've ordered anything we don't already have, and Kendra has arrived with the breast pump, which is a scary-looking contraception and reminds me of when I visited my cousin's dairy farm when I was a kid.

We've also worked out which one of the women will do a night feed so Isla can keep sleeping once she's got the expressing thing.

The meeting ends and the men trail out, heading to the kitchen to find another bacon sandwich.

Raiden slaps me on the back. "You did good, kid."

His praise makes my chest swell. He's been like a father to me since he rescued me from a dark place two years ago, and I'll never be able to repay him for that.

"But she's going to need some time."

I frown at him. Are my feelings that transparent? "It's not like that."

He shakes his head slowly and smiles. "I can see right through you, Luke. You're as protective of her as I was when I met Isabella." A fond smile curls his lips when he thinks of his fiery upstart of a wife. "Just be patient. She'll need time to heal."

I voice the fear that eats at my belly. A fear I could only speak of to Raiden. "But what if she doesn't want me? I'm only half a man. How can I give her what she needs?"

Raiden snorts. "You're more of a man then most men I know, Luke. If she can't see that, then she's not worthy of you."

He squeezes my shoulder, and I'm left wondering if he's right. Could I ever have a chance with Isla? Would it even be fair to her to expect her to be with a man like me?

I shake the thoughts from my head. That doesn't matter now. The important thing is getting Isla help, and with the MC rallying for her, we'll have her catching up on the sleep she needs in no time.

4

ISLA

*M*y eyes flicker open, and the first thing I notice is how quiet it is. I sit up quickly and the basinet is empty. Panic tightens my chest until I remember Danni tiptoeing in at five-thirty this morning and taking the crying Cody from the crib.

She gave me a smile and told me to go back to sleep as she carried him out of the room, his cries getting softer as she moved down the hall.

For the first few mornings I couldn't bear my baby being taken away by strangers, and I worried he wouldn't drink the milk I've been expressing and keeping in bags in the fridge. The first morning I followed Danni down the stairs, sure my baby would need his mother.

But the little guy soon settled, and Danni expertly fed him from a bottle and changed his diaper and kept him entertained with bright plastic toys from a box in the club nursery room. I did not expect a motorcycle club to have a brightly decorated room full of toys for kids of all ages and a nursing chair. Shows how much I know about MCs.

The women have been doing shifts to help, but Danni seems to be the one Cody settles the quickest with.

This is the first morning I've been able to go back to sleep after she takes him, content with the knowledge that my baby is just fine without me for a few hours.

I stretch luxuriously, enjoying the big soft bed and the experience of waking up on my own rather than to Cody's cries.

How long has it been since I got to sleep in? I check my phone and it's just after seven, which is sleeping in for me now that I'm a mother.

There's a message from Ian, and my gut twists when I see his name.

When are you coming back?

I worked up the courage to call Ian two days ago and told him it was over. He yelled at me and told me I was embarrassing him by calling off the wedding, which confirmed I'm doing the right thing.

He never once mentioned he missed me or Cody.

I haven't told him where I am. He's still mad and a mad Ian could be dangerous, especially if I've embarrassed him, which he thinks I have. He's been messaging me ever since.

I put my phone down and try to block out all thoughts of Ian.

Now that I'm getting more sleep, my mind is clearer. I have no doubt I made the right decision to leave. But I need to find a way to support myself and Cody for the long term, and I refuse to go begging to Ian for help.

Which means finding a job, preferably one that will be flexible around looking after my son.

I grab a shower and wash my hair, enjoying taking my time. I shave my legs for the first time in weeks and moisturize them afterwards. I'm not sure who it was that stocked the bathroom cabinet, but I have to find out and thank them. My legs are silky smooth, and I feel like a proper woman for the first time in weeks.

I towel dry my hair, but I've already been too long, so I don't use the hair dryer. I need to get downstairs to see my baby and relieve Danni from her duties.

I still can't believe how kind everyone has been. Luke organized a rotation of help, and all the women are pitching in. I'll never be able to thank them enough.

Which is why I need to find a job and a place to live and get back on my own two feet.

I head downstairs and follow the sounds of children's laughter to the playroom. It's a testament to how family oriented this MC is that they have a room in their HQ that's for kids.

Luke is in his wheelchair with a little boy, Marco, whom I've learned is the club President's son, on his lap. He reads him a story that he's too young to understand but the toddler stares up at Luke in wonder, giggling at the funny voices he makes.

Danni's kids sit on cushions around Luke stacking colorful blocks into towers and knocking them down again.

Cody is asleep in a basinet in the corner.

Luke looks up and catches my eye. It's like an electric shock in my veins whenever he looks at me.

He smiles at me then turns his attention back to the little boy in his lap. Damn, he looks good with a child on his lap.

My chest expands. There are good men in the world. Men that are gentle and kind and still believe women and children should be protected.

The story finishes, and as the boy climbs off Luke's chair he scrambles over Luke's stumps, but if it hurts him, he doesn't show it.

I sneak over to check on Cody, and he's sleeping peacefully.

"He went down about twenty minutes ago." Luke wheels up behind me, and we both look down at my sleeping son. He'll probably sleep for another twenty minutes.

Danni comes into the room. Her hair is in a 1950s roll, and her bright red lipstick is perfectly in place. She doesn't look like a woman who's been up with a baby since five-thirty this morning.

She gives me a warm smile and launches into a report on what Cody ate and what was in his diapers and how long he's been asleep.

She looks down at the crib fondly. "He's a sweet little guy."

"Don't you have your own kids to look after?" I'm worried that I'm imposing too much, that I'll never be able to repay the kindnesses I'm being shown here.

Danni swipes the air in front of me as if shooing away my concerns. "What's one more? I love babies. Kendra will come in soon to help, and Luke is great with kids."

She says the last, giving me a pointed look that makes me blush. Is it that obvious that I'm in awe of the man who's been my savior and my protector since I got here?

Luke moved into the bedroom next to mine upstairs, and I'm pretty sure he spends the nights sleeping in the corridor.

"Did you eat yet?" Luke asks.

He looks concerned, and it amazes me that this stranger is more concerned about my wellbeing than Ian ever was.

"Not yet."

"Go get some breakfast," Danni urges. "I'll bring Cody through when he wakes up."

I follow Luke through to the club kitchen, resisting the urge to get every door for him. I've learned he likes to be independent. So when we get to the kitchen, I sit on a stool and watch as he expertly maneuvers his chair around, grabbing frying pans and bacon and whisking eggs.

The chair catches on the corner of the bench, and Luke curses under his breath as he's jolted from the knock. But he quickly realigns his wheels to take the corner.

I want to ask him about his injury, but I don't know if it's polite. There are so many other things I want to know about this man and how he lost his legs doesn't seem the most important. But the wheelchair seems cumbersome, and I'm sure there must be an easier way.

"Why don't you use prosthetics?"

He frowns into the pan of eggs he's scrambling at a low workstation that I think has been put in just for him, and I wonder if I've crossed a line. He probably doesn't want to talk about it.

"Sorry, it's none of my business. Just curious."

Luke stirs the eggs. "It's fine. I have a set, and I do use them sometimes. But they're uncomfortable. They rub against my skin and itch. I prefer my wheels. I always have."

He grins as he spoons the eggs onto the plate next to a stack of bacon. "There were only two things I was certain of when I was growing up." He holds up two fingers, counting them off. "One, I was going into the military and two, I was going to work with bikes."

He sets a plate down in front of me with toast, scrambled egg and crispy bacon. I'm not gonna lie, a girl could get used to this.

I bite into the bacon, and it crunches under my teeth. I close my eyes and moan, and when I open them, Luke's looking at me funny.

I quickly finish my mouthful. I want to know more about him, and now that I'm getting enough sleep it's like a fog has lifted in my brain, and I'm able to hold a conversation again.

"Why those two things?"

"I loved everything with wheels when I was a kid. I had a stack of toy cars and bikes. I got my first dirt bike when I was six years old and rode it every chance I got. It wasn't long before I started tinkering with it, taking it apart and putting it back together."

His eyes shine when he talks, and I get a glimpse of the carefree boy he once was.

"That's why you're a bike mechanic." Luke already told me he works in the bike shop out the back of the Wild Riders compound. "How about the military?"

"My father was in the military; he served with Raiden." Something dark flashes across his face. "That's how I ended up here."

I cock my head, wanting to know more. I think of the little boy on his lap this morning and how I've seen him reach for Luke with open arms like he was family. "You're close to Raiden and his kids."

"I look after them sometimes when he needs me to and if I'm not working in the garage."

He swallows his mouthful and looks down at his plate, pushing some egg around with his fork.

"I was in a dark place after I came back from Afghanistan." His brow furrows, and for a moment he's back there again. Darkness and pain come into his eyes, and I feel the waves of loss emanating from him.

I lay my hand on his arm. "I'm so sorry. We don't have to talk about it if you don't want to."

He shakes his head as if clearing the memory. "Raiden found me when I was down. He offered me an opportunity here. I don't know where I'd be if he hadn't saved me. I'd do anything for that man."

He says it simply, and I see the fierce loyalty in his statement. He stabs a piece of bacon with his fork and pops it in his mouth.

My heart goes out to this man who gave so much for his country and is still a military man at heart, protecting me and loyal to Raiden.

There are still good men in this world, and I'm being cared for by one of them. My heart flutters in my chest, and I wonder what it would be like to be loved by a man like Luke who's protective and thoughtful, loyal and kind.

But he's just doing his duty. It's obvious he misses the military and having a purpose. Raiden must have told him to look after me, and he's following orders. He said himself that he'd do anything for Raiden.

Besides, what does a single mom with no job and a possibly violent ex have to offer a man like Luke? I'm damaged and broken, and even if he saw me as something more, I'm not good enough for a good man like Luke.

5
ISLA

*T*he next few days pass in the same steady routine. Danni or Maggie or Kendra take it in turns to stay at the clubhouse and come and get Cody for his early feed while I catch up on the sleep I missed during the night and take a shower. Every morning Luke makes me breakfast and we talk over bacon and eggs, which it turns out he knows how to cook to perfection every way you can think of: fried, poached, scrambled, and my favorite, dippy soldiers, which I haven't had since I was a kid.

With three meals a day and six hours of sleep, I've noticed myself growing mentally and physically stronger. I've spent the last two days scanning job sites looking for marketing jobs that I'd be a good fit for. The problem is that they're all based in Charlotte, and when I think about going back to where I've lived with Ian for the last two years, my gut tightens into a knot.

I don't want to go back to the city where I could run

into his family or friends on every corner. He's already started a pity campaign online, playing the victim and making me out to be a bad person for running away. He's been posting all over social media saying he's looking for me and Cody as if I'm some terrible woman who stole his son and not a mother protecting her child from a monster.

I'll have to let him know where I am eventually, or it could turn ugly if the police get involved. But his texts have turned angry, and there's no way I want to see him when he's so volatile.

I've tried to tell him I'll see him once he calms down, but that only adds fuel to the fire, and last night he left an angry voice message yelling at me about how calm he is.

Meanwhile I've broken the news to Mom that the wedding is off. After a lot of protesting and sticking up for Ian, she finally believed me. He's unhinged. He needs help and therapy, and until that happens, I don't want him near Cody.

Mom promised to have a conversation with Malorie, her best friend and Ian's mother. It'll be an awkward conversation, but Malorie has to know what her son's really like. Although I suspect she probably does already.

I'm playing with Cody and some of the other kids in the playroom when Raiden stalks into the room.

His little boy wobbles over to him and he scoops him into his arms, a soft smile on his weatherbeaten face.

"I hear you're looking for a job."

I startle when I realize he's talking to me. I find the thickset brooding club president a little intimidating. I'm not sure if he's hinting it's time for me to leave. Perhaps I've overstayed my welcome.

"I've applied for fifteen in the last few days," I tell him. "I can waitress here if you need help, or clean, or…or…" I search around, wondering what else I could do here. I would offer childcare, but that seems pretty much sewn up.

"Do you know anything about websites?"

I've set up a few for friends, and while the backend isn't my specialty, I can write copy and set out a page. "Yeah, a bit."

"I might have something for you. Come and speak to Barrels."

Twenty minutes later, I step out of Raiden's office with a smile on my face.

I have a job. It's part-time and not many hours to start with, but it will pay for my board and food as long as I want to stay and give me a little extra pocket money.

Barrel's, or Quentin as he's called outside the club, runs the brewery out back. They're expanding the business, and they need extra help on their marketing team. I'll be updating the website, running social media, and anything else they need. And best of all, I'll be doing it from right here with whatever hours suit me. Which means during Cody's nap times, in the evenings, and anytime during the day when someone's around to mind Cody.

It's perfect and means I don't have to hurry to make a decision about where I want to be permanently until I'm ready.

I'm so excited my first thought is to tell Luke. After checking on Cody, I head out to the bike shop across the parking lot.

Luke isn't there, and Colter, Danni's husband, tells me he's working out at the club gym.

I head back inside and down the stairs to the basement gym. As I descend the stairs, the smell of sweat and vinyl reaches my nose. Weights clank and soft grunts reach my ears. I hang back, suddenly nervous about entering this masculine domain.

Luke is on the bench with his wheelchair discarded next to it. His shirt is off, and muscles ripple across his torso. I stop in the doorway, and my heart clangs against my rib cage. He's doing sit-ups at an impressive pace, and every time he sits up his muscles ripple, making the tattoo across his chest dance.

I'm reminded of the first time I saw him here in this room and the jolt that went through me, how my knees went wobbly and I thought it was from lack of sleep. But as I watch Luke relentlessly work his upper body, my knees weaken, my throat goes dry, and damp heat pools in my panties. My core tightens, and a yearning that I haven't felt for months tugs at me.

I vaguely notice the stumps of his limbs sticking out from his exercise shorts, but they don't matter. They're a curious distraction to the vision of this muscular man pushing himself to the limit. His eyes are squeezed shut, and he counts under his breath with every sit-up.

"Ninety-six, ninety-seven, ninety-eight…"

His voice turns to a grunt and his body wavers. I hold my breath as he pushes up again.

"Ninety-nine…" He pauses on the bench with his head just off it, then his grunt turns to a groan as he strains up one last time. "One hundred."

Luke falls back onto the bench, and his body relaxes in relief. He loosens the strap around his lower body, and his stump thumps on the bench.

I remember the first day I saw him and how he looked away in embarrassment as my eyes traveled down his body.

I've gotten to know Luke over the last week, and I barely notice his missing limbs or the fact that he's in a wheelchair. He's just Luke, the kind, funny, and protective man who I'm starting to have feelings for. He wouldn't want anyone to see him like this, panting on the bench while his missing limbs twitch.

I drag my gaze away from his toned muscles and slip away. My news will have to wait.

Later that night, long after I've put Cody down after his late feed, I roll over in bed, unable to get comfortable. My mind goes back to Luke, to his rippling muscles, to the perspiration flying off him and to the masculine smell of the gym, ripe with sweat and determination.

I wonder what it would feel like to have those arms pin me down, to have his stubble scrape against my thighs.

It's been a long time since a man touched me. Ian was

turned off ever since I got pregnant, and I didn't miss his awkward fumbling.

Now, a yearning grows in my lower belly that's so strong I squeeze my thighs together. My hands brush over my breasts, swollen and sensitive from nursing. I carry on over my belly and between my legs.

I gasp at the sensation, and as my fingers slide over my damp panties I imagine it's Luke's hand. I imagine he's lying here next to me with his hard chest pressed against me and his hands exploring my intimate parts.

As I slide into my panties and relieve the ache in my core, I imagine it's Luke taking care of me in one more way. And as I sink into pleasure, I imagine it's him who whispers to me to stay, to stay on Wild Heart Mountain with him.

6

LUKE

*S*omething startles me awake, and my chair rattles as I jolt in my seat. I peer into the darkness of the corridor and hear it again.

Footsteps.

Someone's creeping up the clubhouse stairs. I roll the blanket off my shoulders and drop it silently to the floor. I don't want it getting in the way if I have to launch myself at anyone.

Slowly I turn my chair around to face the corridor and stretch my arms out, flexing my muscles. If Isla's asshole ex has come for her, he's going to get a hell of a surprise.

The stairs creak, and a curly haired head comes into view.

Maggie gasps when she sees me at the end of the corridor wide awake and glaring at her.

"What the fuck, Luke?" she hisses, keeping her voice low. "You gave me a heart attack."

"What are you sneaking around for?" I try to keep my voice low, but the adrenaline is still pumping.

Isla says Ian doesn't know where she is, but his texts are getting more and more erratic. The guy hasn't accepted her decision to leave him yet.

"I came to check on Cody. I haven't heard any cries yet, and he's usually awake by now."

I check my watch and it's six-thirty a.m. It's hard to tell it's morning when it's still dark outside. Usually Cody's cries wake me up at about the same time that Danni or Maggie or Kendra arrives to take the morning shift.

But he's quiet this morning.

"Do you think he's okay?" Maggie looks anxious. "You spend all the time wanting them to sleep through, but when they do it scares the shit out of you."

She gives a nervous laugh, but I'm not taking any chances. "I'll take a look."

I open the door more carelessly than I should if there's a sleeping baby, but the silence has me rattled.

Without trying to be quiet, I wheel up to the basinet as fast as I can. My heart's racing as I peer over the top of the basinet.

Cody's laying on his back with one arm thrown over his head. I lean forward as far as I can until I see his little chest rising and falling and I'm satisfied he's breathing.

Maggie has come up next to me, and we give each other a relieved smile.

He's sleeping. He's finally sleeping past five thirty.

I glance over at Isla. The glow from the nightlight bathes the room in a golden light, giving her a warm glow. She sleeps on her side facing the basinet, her body curled tight and her hair falling over the pillow behind her. My breath catches at the sight of her, so fucking beautiful.

Her mouth is open, and even in sleep there's a slight frown on her face.

I long to climb into the bed with her. To wrap my arms around her body and pull her close. But she's not mine to touch, and even if she was, how strange would it feel for her if she nuzzled back into me and found only half a man behind her.

I turn around awkwardly in the small space and follow Maggie out of the room. She closes the door quietly behind us.

"I'll go put a pot of coffee on and start prepping the kitchen." Maggie's the pastry chef here at the Wild Taste Restaurant, which is part of the club HQ. She's been doing the early shifts with Cody to coincide with her work shifts.

She looks as pleased as I do that Cody's still asleep. I may not have babies of my own, but I've spent the last two weeks since Isla and Cody turned up reading everything I can about them. So I know what a triumph it is when they sleep through the night.

"You want a coffee?" Maggie asks.

I shake my head. "I'll stay up here." I'm rattled from earlier, thinking it might have been Ian on the stairs. "I'll text you when he wakes."

Maggie heads downstairs, and I turn my chair around to take up position outside of Isla's room.

Isla may think Ian won't find her, but I know what desperate men will do. I'm not taking any chances.

It's not until almost seven that Cody wakes, and by then Isla gets up with him. I retreat into my room when I hear them moving about. I moved into the room next to Isla's for as long as she's here. It's the one Raiden had renovated to accommodate my wheelchair, so I'd always have a place to crash if I needed it.

I have my own ground level apartment in Wild, but I stayed here for a few weeks when I first joined the club. It's just one more thing I'm grateful to Raiden for.

My apartment is a rental, but I've been saving my money and working on designs for an accessible cabin. I'm planning to start the build this spring and need to finalize the plans.

I head downstairs for coffee with my designs and spread them on the table. It's all one level with one large bedroom and a home gym.

But for the first time I wonder if I'll need extra bedrooms.

It took me a long time to accept my disability and my new way of moving through life. But once I did, I was determined not to let it slow me down. I've adapted a motorbike, I've pushed myself at the gym, I've been on every charity run with the club since I got patched. I've got a good life here.

A single life.

Until a few weeks ago, I was fine with that. I'd resigned myself to living a bachelor life, because what woman would want me? And I hadn't met a woman that sparked my interest anyway.

A few times Arlo dragged me out to the White Out club or the rougher Wild Times bar in Wild which has no ramp, so I have to wear my prosthetics and be uncomfortable all night. But all I see is pity in the eyes of the women who bother to talk to me.

Arlo says I should use that, that some women are willing to do anything to thank returning servicemen. But I don't want to be anyone's pity fuck, and I don't need thanks for serving. It was my duty to serve this country, and I didn't do it to pick up women.

But here's the truth. I don't know if I can be with a woman. My dick still works, and it's been hard a hell of a lot since Isla walked into the clubhouse.

But the thought of being intimate with a woman makes me nervous. How can I be naked, how can I show my mangled stumps of legs without turning a woman off?

I couldn't handle seeing the horror in a woman's eyes when the reality of what I hide under my specially tailored slacks is exposed.

Better the single life for me.

I crumple up the piece of paper with my crude design for my cabin. I won't be needing those extra rooms. An accessible kitchen, bathroom, bedroom and gym. That's all this single man needs.

. . .

It's later in the day, and I've been working out in the repair shop. I like to come in during my lunch break to check on Isla and Cody. As I come in the back door, I hear women's laughter from the office. It sounds like Isla; I've heard her laugh a couple of times but never as carefree as this.

My chair catches on the doorframe as I go through the almost too narrow doorway, and I graze my knuckles. Ignoring the pain I wheel to the office, wondering what she's finding so funny.

Isla sits in an office chair with a laptop open on the desk in front of her. Bit Rate leans over her furiously clicking the keys. Their heads are almost touching.

My stomach tightens as jealousy courses through me.

"What are you doing?" I grit out.

Isla startles at my abrupt tone, and her hand flies to her chest. "Luke, you scared me."

I turn my scowl to Bit Rate. He should know better than to be in here flirting with Isla. He's just confessed his love to his nanny. He should be at home with her and not here hanging over Isla.

He raises his eyebrows at me, looking amused.

"I'm getting Isla's laptop set up." His amused look turns to a grin, and I get the feeling he can see right through me. He holds his hands up in the air and steps away from her. "You okay with that? Or does it need to go on the schedule?"

He's teasing me, but I can't stop the thundering of my

heart. Isla looks between us with a frown on her face, and the last thing I want to do is upset her. She told me she had a job helping Barrels with marketing and Bit Rate does the club IT, so it seems legit.

"What schedule?" Isla asks.

Bit Rate's grin widens, and he's enjoying this. "Didn't Luke tell you? He organized a schedule to make sure there was always someone on hand to look after Cody."

Isla turns to me. "That was you?"

I look away. It's too painful to see the appreciation in her eyes. If I was any other man, she might throw her arms around me and I'd sweep her off her feet. But I'll never be that man.

"Of course it was him," says Bit Rate. "He's the one who asked Barrels about the job too."

I cut Bit Rate a look, because I didn't want Isla to know I've done this all for her. She might feel weird about it.

But when I glance at her, there are tears in her eyes. "Luke," she whispers, "that's the kindest thing anyone's ever done for me."

"It's nothing," I mumble. I want to say I'd do it for anyone, but I don't know if that's true.

I'm saved from the awkward situation by the sounds of Cody crying somewhere down the hall. Isla pushes her chair back. "It's time for his next feed."

As she brushes past me, she touches my shoulder. I glance up at her and our eyes lock. "Thank you." She leans down, and her lips brush against my cheek.

It's a friendly kiss, a thank you kiss. But I close my

eyes and breathe in deep, savoring her scent of milk and lavender and baby powder.

When I open my eyes, Isla's gone and Bit Rate's, staring at me shaking his head slowly from side to side. "Are you going to make a move or just moon over her for another two weeks?"

"I don't know what you mean."

He snort laughs. "You've had it bad since she turned up, Luke. And I get it, she's dealing with a situation, but it's been two weeks, man. It's obvious to everyone how you feel about her. You got everyone in the club running after this woman. And you know why we're doing it? Because we all know she's going to be your old lady. So put us all out of our misery and make it official, please."

He's half teasing, but he doesn't understand. I glance down at my lap and the useless stumps where legs should be. "I can't."

Bit Rate pulls out the chair and maneuvers it around until he's facing me. "What's holding you back?"

I snort laugh, because he must be joking. "In case you haven't noticed, I'm missing both my legs and I'm in a wheelchair."

Bit Rate winces. "You think Isla gives a shit about that?"

"Of course she does. No woman wants half a man. No matter how good a person they are."

"Luke, you're sleeping outside her room, you're feeding her every day, you've organized a team to help her with the baby, and you got her a job. If she's worried about a few missing limbs, then I've read her all wrong and she doesn't deserve you."

He's gone from teasing to earnest. "Trust me, what women really want is a kind heart, someone who supports them, and blind devotion. If you can give her those things, then she'll give them right back. And when that happens…" He sits back and smiles, no doubt thinking about Freya. "…it's a beautiful thing. Take it from this old man. If you have a chance, you've got to grasp it with both hands."

He makes it sound so easy. But I've never had a serious relationship before. Even if Isla was interested, I have no idea where to begin.

"How?"

Bit Rate leans back in his chair. "Take her out, have some fun. Show her who you are and make her remember she's a woman and not just a mom."

What he's saying makes sense. Maybe if Isla really knew me, she could see past the chair, past what's missing. But what if she can't?

"I'm scared."

Bit Rate chuckles. "We're all fucking scared when we find the woman we love. But just remember, you can face down anything. The enemy did their worst to you, and you survived. You're a badass motherfucker, Luke. Now go out there and get your girl."

7
ISLA

*C*ody suckles contentedly on my breast as I cradle him in my arms, rocking gently in the feeding chair in the corner of the playroom.

I run a hand over his downy head, and my heart fills with wonder at this tiny miracle. I've felt this way ever since he was born, intense feelings of love combined with exhaustion and fear.

"We're going to be okay."

For the first time, I believe the words I whisper to him. I have a job, a place to stay, and a way forward. I won't be able to live at the clubhouse forever, but if I can prove myself in the job and extend the hours, I should be able to get a place on my own in a few months.

Luke says I need to push Ian for child support, but I'm not ready to have that conversation yet. One of the guys here is a lawyer, and Luke has already put him in touch in case things get tricky with Ian and we have to go through the courts.

My instinct is to not take anything from Ian. But I won't be able to afford childcare if I don't. I can't rely on the women of the club forever.

The air in the room shifts, and before I even hear the soft turn of his wheels, I know Luke is here. As usual he ducks his head, averting his eyes while I feed even though I've told him a hundred times it doesn't bother me. I'm feeding my baby, and it's nothing to be ashamed about.

"Danni's going to take Cody for a few hours when you're finished."

I frown at his words. I usually spend the afternoon with my son. The women here do enough, and I can't expect them to have him all the time. "Do they need me to work?"

"No. I'm taking you out."

A thrill goes through me at his words. I can't remember the last time I went anywhere without Cody. But he's become such a part of me I don't know if I can. "I can't leave him."

"Yes you can. For two hours, that's all." There's a determined expression on Luke's face, making me wonder what he's got planned. I still can't believe it was him that organized the women into a schedule and spoke to Barrels about the job. He's done so much for me and I'll never be able to repay him, although I can think of a few ways I'd like to.

I still can't get the image out of my mind of Luke's muscles straining as he works out. He's sex on wheels, and he doesn't even know it.

I glance down at my baby, my world. He's been my sole focus since he was born six weeks ago. I guess it can't hurt to leave him for a few hours. He's gotten used to Danni, and once he's fed, he'll be ready for a sleep.

"I'll get Cody down first."

Luke nods. "I'll meet you out front."

"Where are we going?" I don't have any clothes apart from the few things I came with. They've been fine for lounging around the clubhouse, but I have no idea what Luke has planned.

He grins. "It's a surprise. Wear your jeans and a sweater. I've got a jacket for you."

Twenty minutes later, I follow Luke out the back of the clubhouse and across the parking lot to the bike shop.

This is where Luke works. I've visited him before when I take Cody out for walks. Usually he's on the adapted rolling platform that means he can keep low to the ground and work on the bikes that come into the garage.

Today he's waiting next to his adapted bike. It's a beautiful-looking contraption. The bike is a Harley with thick wheels and low handlebars. Luke's attached a side carriage with a fold down ramp.

"Welcome to my chariot." He grins when he sees my expression.

"We're going on the bike?"

"Yup. I'm taking you out for a ride." He holds up his Wild Riders MC jacket. "Put this on." I take the leather jacket off him and slide it on over my sweater. It smells like leather and bike grease and a rich scent that's all Luke.

"I'll get on first." He rolls up the ramp, and with quick movements pulls himself out of the chair and onto the motorbike.

He leans over and folds his chair up, securing it in place with safety ties.

Along the side of the bike and the side attachment are painted red and orange flames. I can see why Luke got the road name Chariot. He looks like a Roman god sitting tall and proud.

"Come on up." He gestures for me to get on, and a thrill snakes down my spine and there's a tug on my core.

I can't believe I get to ride next to this man, the proud warrior.

I climb onto the side extension, and Luke pulls a lever to raise the ramp behind me. There's a folded down seat and I go to pull it open, but Luke puts a hand on my arm to stop me.

"You're riding on the back." He indicates the seat of the bike directly behind him.

My pulse kicks up a notch as I slide onto the bike behind Luke. There's no way to not touch him as I wiggle into place. My hips snap into place behind him, and my chest pushes up against his back.

There's a lot of me, and he might not have considered how cozy this was going to be when he suggested I ride pillion.

"Put your arms around me, Isla."

Or maybe he did. I've seen the way Luke looks at me and the kindness he's shown. When I first arrived I was too caught up in my own situation to notice, but over the last week, I've noticed Luke very much.

And when I slide my arms around his waist, I notice the little sigh of pleasure that matches my own. It feels good to touch him, to breathe in his scent of leather and bike grease. I bump up against his hard back, and for the first time in a long time, it feels like there's something solid holding me up.

Luke starts the engine, and we cruise out of the parking lot. Bit Rate comes out of the club headquarters grinning like a fool and waves us off.

We take it slowly, heading further up the mountain on the windy roads. The snow from Christmas has cleared, but the air is cold, and I snuggle against Luke for warmth.

As we ride further away from the clubhouse and from my baby, I begin to remember that other part of me. That part that isn't just a mother feeding and caring for her newborn. The part of me that's a woman clinging onto the back of a hot guy on a motorbike.

We ride for about twenty minutes before Luke turns down a dirt road. We take it slowly until the road opens out onto a small parking lot and a picnic area.

It's empty today, but I bet come summer it's full of tourists. The view is stunning. It looks over the valley and a sea of green treetops. Some of them still have a dusting of white snow.

There's a grassy area with picnic tables, and a path winds its way to a stack of large boulders.

Luke parks the bike, and I reluctantly slide off. A cold shiver goes through me at the loss of his body heat.

Luke wheels himself off the bike and opens the saddle bag and pulls out a blanket. He puts it on his knee and we take the path to the boulders. The ground is uneven, but I know better than to ask Luke if he needs help.

We stop at the boulders and Luke angles his chair right up close. He fists his hands and puts them on the boulder, then hauls himself up.

I can see why he spends so much time at the gym. His upper body strength is incredible. I scramble up next to him and shiver as the cool air hits me.

"Here. Come in close." He wraps the blanket around both our shoulders, and for a while we sit in silence looking out at the valley. Just two people enjoying the view.

Luke twitches, and his face screws up in a wince.

"What is it? Are you okay?"

"Yeah." He reaches under the blanket and presses on the end of his stump. "I get phantom pain sometimes. It's been over two years, and my brain still thinks I have legs."

I can't imagine what that's like, trying to scratch an itch that's not really there.

"How did it happen?"

We've talked a lot in the past few weeks, but Luke's never mentioned what happened. He doesn't answer for a long time, and I worry I've crossed a line.

"You don't need to answer."

"It's fine." He looks down at his lap and tugs on the corner of the blanket. "I was a bike mechanic in the army. That made my mother less anxious, the fact that I wasn't on the frontline."

He chuckles, but it's a hollow laugh. "I was in a convoy moving between bases, and we hit an IED. Next thing I remember is waking up in a hospital bed in Germany. I don't remember anything about the explosion or how I got out. Everyone kept telling me I was one of the lucky ones."

He shrugs. "For a long time I didn't feel lucky. I was in a dark place until Raiden dragged me out of it. He served with my father, and my old man asked him to meet me. Raiden offered me a place here with the MC. A job, a new start."

Luke turns to look at me, and his eyes blaze with fierce loyalty. "He saved my life."

"You're loyal." It's a nice quality. "I wish all men were as loyal as you."

I'm thinking about Ian and how it's only when I left that he cared about me.

"Do you miss him? Your ex?" Luke asks as if reading my mind.

I think about Ian, and all I feel is a sense of freedom. "No. I should have left a long time ago. I don't know why I didn't. I was scared of what he would do and embarrassed."

I look down at my hands and pull at a loose bit of

nail. "I don't know how I got into that kind of relationship. I'm a smart woman; how did it happen to me?"

Luke takes my hand. "Don't be so hard on yourself, Isla."

His hands are cold, and I run my fingers over them. There's grease under his fingernails and the skin on his knuckles is scraped raw over hard calluses. It's a reminder of his grit and determination. I've seen him getting himself around by hauling himself up on his fists. What kind of man is tough enough to break the skin on his knuckles, let them heal, and break them again and again and again?

"I don't even think about Ian," I confess. "It's a relief not to have him in my life. I don't want to think about him now." My heart's hammering in my chest, and I glance up at Luke to find him staring at me.

His gaze flicks to my lips. "I want you to be selfish for a little while, Isla, I want you only to think about yourself."

Then his lips are on mine, firm yet gentle and with a tenderness that brings tears to my eyes. This is how I need to be kissed; this is how I need to be loved.

"Let me take care of you," Luke whispers against my lips, and my body sparks to life as I surrender to him.

8

LUKE

*I*sla sighs into my mouth and relaxes against me. She tastes like mint and milk and heaven all rolled into one.

Her hair falls across her face, tickling my chin, and the caress makes my dick harden. It's been too long since I kissed a woman and her lips on mine are overwhelming, making me feel dizzy.

Cool air whips around us, but it does nothing to cool my heated body. My lips tingle from heat, and my skin is on fire.

The kiss turns hungry as my need for her grows. I grasp Isla with both hands, sliding my fingers through her hair to grip her head and hold her to me.

Her hands snake under my jacket, and she trails her hand down my chest and over my torso. Everywhere she touches my skin turns to fire. I groan into her mouth and shuffle forward to press myself against her.

Her hands run over my package and the groan turns to a growl. My dick jerks into her palm, and I pull away.

Cold mountain air gushes into the space between us, and everything crashes around me. I can't touch this woman like I want to. I have no claim on her.

Isla's brows knit together in confusion. "What's wrong?" Her hand rests lightly over the top of my jeans, applying gentle pressure on my cock.

I'm breathing hard, trying to pull back from the abyss that one touch almost had me falling over. "You don't need to do that."

She pulls her hand away, looking hurt. "I want to."

"You don't need to thank me like that, Isla."

She looks like she's been slapped. "You think this is what this is?"

I close my eyes, annoyed that I even said that. "I don't know what this is. I only know you're confused. You've got a baby, and you've just left an emotionally abusive relationship. You don't need me confusing the issue."

"I'm not confused, Luke. It's over with Ian if that's what you're worried about."

I wish that was all I was worried about. I open my eyes to find Isla frowning at me. I've thoroughly fucked this up. I wanted to take her out for a while, and now I'm saying shit like a fucking idiot when I should have kept my mouth shut and just kissed her. But if we kept kissing, I would have embarrassed myself.

"It's been a long time since I was with a woman, Isla, not since before the accident. You touch me like that, and I'll go off like a rocket."

63

Relief floods her face, and she giggles. "Is that all? I thought you didn't like me."

"Didn't like you?" I want to tell her I love her, that I've loved her since she walked in the clubhouse door and stole my heart. But I don't want to scare her away. "That's not it."

I also can't admit my real fear. That I'm not man enough for her. That if we take this further, I'll embarrass myself. That I won't be the lover she needs. I have no idea if I can please a woman or not anymore or even how the mechanics of making love work when you don't have the counterbalance of legs to work with. I might not be able to please her, and I want more than anything to please Isla.

"We're going to keep this real simple. To make this less confusing, I'm going to take myself out of the equation."

Isla bites her lower lip and a blush creeps up her neck. I trail my finger over her cheek and cup her chin.

"Since you walked into my club, it's been my mission to look after you and Cody. To make sure you're safe, to make sure you're sleeping and eating and recovering. Let me look after you now, like a man looks after a woman."

My hand trails down her neck, and I squeeze her throat a little on the way down to her chest. Isla gasps, and her eyes widen. I want to own her, to possess her, and maybe one day I will, but today all I'm going to do is make her forget her troubles for a little while. Make her remember she's a woman and what it feels like to come undone.

I slowly unzip the leather jacket she's wearing, and every ping of the zipper echoes around the quiet valley.

Her chest rises and falls in heaving breaths as I nudge the jacket aside and slide one hand around her waist. The other hand trails over the curves of her body to cup her breast. She shudders at my touch as I cup her heavy breast in my palm.

"Are they sensitive?" I long to tear her top off and explore her perfect breasts, but I've read about how sensitive they can be when a woman is breastfeeding.

She nods, and I pray to the gods I get another opportunity to explore them properly as I slide my hands down her body and between her legs. Isla gasps, and her mouth pops open.

"Is this okay?"

It's been so long since I touched a woman like this, and I don't want to fuck it up.

"Luke..." she whines, "it's perfect."

I nudge her thighs apart and caress the hot place between her legs. I can't feel much through her jeans, but Isla whimpers and rests her hand behind her so she's leaning back on the boulder.

Her jeans have an elastic waist, and I slide my hands down them. Her underwear is soaked, and she whimpers when I touch her.

"Oh baby girl, you've needed this, haven't you?"

"Yes." She bites her lower lip and glances around the empty rest area. "What if someone comes?"

"The boulders shield us from the road, and no one's coming here on a fucking freezing day in January."

She giggles, and it turns into a moan as I find her sensitive core.

"The only person who's going to come is you. Sit back and enjoy it."

I kiss her neck, and she turns to me. Perspiration beads on her forehead, and her eyes are pools of desire. My dick aches for her, and I feel a yearning so strong to be a fucking normal man to be able to give her everything she needs. But this will have to do.

I caress her slick center, keeping my movements slow and controlled, reading her expression to figure out what she likes.

"Luke…" Every time she whimpers my name my chest squeezes.

My lips find hers, and she kisses me hungrily as my hand moves inside her.

She breaks away as it becomes too much, leaning against the rock, and her eyes roll into the back of her head. She squeezes around my fingers and cries my name as the climax consumes her, her body releasing the tension she's been carrying around for too long.

"You're beautiful." She turns her face to me, and her eyes are hooded. The moment we make eye contact, I press against her center, and she cries out. I drag her over the edge again and again until she's a trembling mess against me.

Only then do I slide out of her panties and enfold her in my arms. She leans again my chest with a contended sigh.

We stay like this for a long moment, and it's only after

a long silence when I look down at her do I realize she's fallen fast asleep.

I brush a strand of hair off her face and hold her tighter. For this moment, Isla is mine. Even if it can't be forever, I have this moment.

9

ISLA

*I*t's been three days since Luke took me for a ride on the back of the bike and reminded me I'm a woman and not just a mom.

Every time he's near me, my body tingles at the memory. I long for him to touch me again, but I don't know how to ask.

Today I'm sitting in a corner of the restaurant with the laptop that Nate, or Bit Rate as the guys call him, set up for me to work from.

Although I'm not getting any work done today. Danni brought Cody through a little while ago. He's fussy and won't settle and wouldn't stop crying until she handed him over to me.

I press my hand to his forehead, but there's no temperature.

"What's got you worked up, little guy?" I kiss the top of his downy head, and he nuzzles into me. I've been spending more time working recently, and maybe he just misses his mommy. I close the laptop lid. I can work later while he's having his nap. For whatever reason Cody needs me today, and that's fine by me.

He only fed an hour ago, but I undo my maternity top to see if he's hungry. He finds my breast and latches on, and that seems to calm him. It still amazes me that I can nourish my baby and provide comfort for him through my boobs. I've learned a new appreciation for my body over the last several months.

I glance at the clock behind the bar, and my stomach flutters. It's almost noon, which means Luke will come in from the garage soon, and we'll eat together. It's become our routine over the last few weeks, and I look forward to it. Conversation flows easily with Luke and he makes me laugh, which I hadn't done a lot of before I got here.

I'm a different woman than the one who turned up here a few weeks ago, scared and embarrassed. Now I've got a job and a place to stay, and the women have become friends. And I've got Luke, although I have no idea what that means. He hasn't kissed me again since we went out on the bike. I don't know what he's thinking or what he feels. I don't know if he's just being kind or if he has feelings for me.

Maybe he's holding back to give me time, or maybe it's something to do with his disability. But I don't see the disability when I'm with Luke. I just see the man. Maybe it's because he's adapted so well. He's patient with himself and never complains. The clubhouse has been adapted to be accessible. He's at home here, and it's starting to feel like my home too.

"For God's sake, Isla, put your tits away."

My head jerks up at the familiar voice. My blood turns cold as Ian strides across the room.

Cody senses the change in me, and he unlatches. My breast flops out of the bra, and I scramble to push it back into the fabric and re-fasten it. My cheeks heat under Ian's look of disgust, and Cody starts to cry.

"What are you doing here?" I try to keep my voice steady, but seeing Ian again brings up memories of him smashing the glass above our heads, his grip on my wrist that left bruises, the disgusted look on his face that became a permanent feature once I became pregnant.

I thought he'd given up looking for me. But somehow he's managed to track me down.

"What the fuck are *you* doing here is the real question." He looks around the clubhouse, and the disgusted look on his face turns to a scowl as his gaze runs over the bike paraphernalia on the walls and the vintage Harley in the corner. "A fucking motorcycle club," he hisses. "You're not safe here."

I bark out a laugh, and it's high-pitched and hysterical. I've never felt so safe in my life.

"How did you find me?"

Ian smirks. "Your mother is concerned. Her and my mom want to know when we're going to make up and get on with the wedding."

I close my eyes and take a deep breath. Typical Mom. Ian's managed to charm her around to his side.

"There won't be a wedding, Ian. You must see we're

not suited to each other. You'll be happier with someone else."

He takes a step forward, so he's towering over me. "I'll be happy when you stop embarrassing me and come back home where you belong." Cody cries, and I hold him close to my chest against my racing heart. My hands tremble as fear shoots through me. "And shut that fucking baby up."

"You need to back the fuck up."

Relief floods me at the sound of Luke's voice. My eyes dart to the back of the restaurant as Luke maneuvers toward me. He's moving as fast as he can and he knocks a table, sending a wine glass smashing to the floor.

Ian spins around and smirks when he sees Luke. "Who the fuck are you?"

Luke stops in front of Ian. "I'm the guy who's going to kick your ass if you don't back the fuck away from Isla and Cody."

Ian laughs, a hollow sound. "You?" He steps back and makes a show of checking out Luke and the wheelchair. "What you gonna do, cripple? Run me over?"

Luke's breathing hard and a vein pulses in his neck. "Try me, motherfucker."

He slides off his Wild Riders MC leather jacket and folds it over the back of a chair. He's wearing a black tank top underneath, and he flexes his muscles, but Ian's too stupid to notice. All he sees is a man in a wheelchair. He can't see past that to the determination and the grit that fuels Luke. He can't see what I see, the loyal, protective, and devoted man who will do anything for me and

Cody. Suddenly the only person I'm scared for is Ian, and that fucker deserves everything that's coming to him.

There's movement in the back of the restaurant as Arlo, Davis, and some of the other guys come into the room.

"You need a hand with this, Luke?" Arlo asks.

Without taking his eyes off Ian, Luke shakes his head. "I got this."

Ian narrows his eyes and chuckles. "You should take the help from your buddies cripple; I don't want to hurt you."

"Isla," Luke speaks slowly through gritted teeth. "Take Cody and go out back."

I push my chair back, and Ian reaches out a hand to grab me. I dodge out of the way and the chair falls to the floor, making Cody howl louder.

"You make a move Isla, and I swear to god I'll hurt this cripple."

I pause as blood thunders in my ears. Ian is mean, and he's a bully. He could hurt Luke badly, and I don't want to be the cause of that. I'm frozen on the spot, unsure what to do.

I glance at Luke, and he gives me a small nod. "I can handle myself. Go stand with Arlo."

Our eyes lock and I see determination there, and I understand. He needs to do this. Even if he gets hurt, he needs to protect me, to know he tried.

I clutch the wailing Cody to my chest and scurry to the back of the restaurant. Arlo puts a protective hand on my shoulder and guides me behind him. But I'm not going to miss whatever happens next. I stand with the line of men, feeling confident knowing they're here for me.

"Isla," Ian thunders, "you're responsible for this. I'm going to fuck up your cripple boyfriend."

Luke grabs the edges of his chair so tight his knuckles turn white. "You get one shot, motherfucker. You better make it a good one."

Ian chuckles then lunges forward. At the same time, Luke pushes himself out of the chair and uses the momentum to throw himself at Ian. There's a look of surprise on Ian's face, and then they tumble to the ground in a flurry of grunts and punches.

Ian should have the advantage, but within seconds Luke has him pinned to the ground. Ian kicks wildly, trying to shake him off with his legs. But Luke clings on and then head butts Ian in the face.

Ian screams as blood spurts out of his nose. He clutches it and starts crying, begging for Luke to stop. But Luke doesn't stop. His hand grips Ian's throat, and the muscles in his arms bulge as he applies pressure.

I start forward, certain Luke's going to kill him. But Arlo and Davis get there first. It takes both of them to pull Luke off.

Ian scrambles backward, clutching his nose as blood spurts onto his crisp white shirt. "You fucker."

Luke grins at him. "You better run, motherfucker, before I get back in my chair to chase you."

Ian scrambles to his feet, his eyes wide with terror. He looks around wildly until he sees me. "Fuck this, Isla.

You're not worth it. You had your chance. The wedding's off."

He turns to Luke, who even from the floor manages to look menacing. "You're welcome to her and the fucking kid."

I hand Cody over to Danni and step forward.

"You're damn right the wedding's off. I don't want you near my son. If you try to come here again, I'll get a restraining order."

"You think I want that screaming baby? It's probably not even mine. You and the cripple are welcome to him."

My eyes are on Luke, and I see him wince at the words. He just kicked Ian's ass in a fight, and Ian still only sees a guy in a wheelchair.

"Happy fucking families. Enjoy life with half a man." The words make me gasp. Luke looks like he's been punched in the guts, and I know that hit home.

10

LUKE

*H*alf a man…cripple…the words lodge in my brain and make my chest ache.

Arlo claps me on the back. "That was awesome, man. I knew you were a badass."

But the praise does nothing to dislodge the pain in my chest. Because as much as I hate the motherfucker, Ian's right. Isla deserves more than a man like me. She deserves the fucking world. Not a man who can't even get himself up off the floor unassisted.

I haul myself over to my chair, but I already know I can't pull myself into it.

Isla comes over, her face full of concern. "Are you okay?"

"Yeah." I try to smile, but I don't want her to witness this. I don't want her to see Arlo and Davis lifting me into my chair.

"Are *you* okay?" I ask.

She crouches in front of me. "I'm shaken, but I'll be fine. He won't come back."

"Not if he knows what's good for him," Arlo says.

Isla reaches out a hand and touches my cheek. It's tender and makes me wince. Ian got a couple of swipes at me before I pinned him down.

"Let me patch you up." Her touch is tender, and I long to lean into it. To feel her caress on my skin and to kiss her again.

"Ready to get back in the chair?" Arlo asks. The question crashes me back to reality. It reminds me of what I lack. I'm half a man. That's all I'll ever be.

"I'll be fine." I jerk my head away from Isla's touch, and confusion and pain flash across her face. "Go tend to Cody."

"Luke…?"

I can't look at her, and I keep my head turned away until she stands up with a sigh. I wait until she's taken Cody out of the room before I allow Arlo and Davis to lift me under the arms and haul me into my chair.

I can't even get off the fucking floor without help. Ian's words ring in my ears.

Half a man, a cripple.

Isla deserves so much more than that.

It's after nine later that night, and I'm in my room when there's a soft knock at the door. I open it to find Isla on the other side with a baby monitor in her hand. She's wearing a loose shirt with milk stains on it, and her hair is in a messy top knot. But she still takes my breath away.

"Can I come in?"

"Sure." I wheel into the room and spin around to face her as she closes the door.

She fidgets with the baby monitor. "Thank you for today. For standing up for me."

I shrug. "I told you I'd protect you, Isla. I just wasn't sure I really could."

She grins. "You were badass Luke. The look on Ian's face when you launched yourself at him." She chuckles. "He wasn't expecting that."

I can't help grinning. I haven't had to test my strength since I've been in the chair. It felt good to know I can take a man down when I need to. "He threatened you."

Isla looks down at the baby monitor and bites her lower lip. "Did I do something wrong?"

Her words cut, and I wheel over so I'm sitting before her. "What makes you say that?"

She looks up at me and her eyes shine, and I hate it that I've hurt her.

She takes a big breath. "I like you, Luke. I like you a lot and I thought you felt the same, but you've been distant, and I don't know what I've done wrong or if I've read the situation wrong…"

She trails off and looks down at her hands.

"Oh honey, it's not you."

"Then what's the problem, Luke?"

I run a hand through my hair. Is she going to make me spell it out? "Look at me, Isla." I wheel a few feet back and hold my arms up. I want her to really see me. "I'm in a wheelchair; I'm missing half my body. You deserve better than that. You deserve a man who's whole."

My voice comes out bitter, and I expect her to nod and leave. I expect her to understand. What I don't expect is the raised eyebrow look she gives me.

"Is that it?" She folds her arms in front of her chest. "Do you think I'm that stupid that I don't see the man you are inside? You think all I see is a man in a wheelchair? That couldn't be further from the truth. I don't see a man in a wheelchair. I see a man. A man with a big heart, who's kind and loyal and determined. A man who launched himself at another man to protect me and my son."

She crouches before me and takes my hands in hers. Her touch is soft, and it eases something in my chest.

"You think you know what I need, Luke? I'll tell you what I need. It's you, Luke. I need you."

My chest expands, and I dare to hope I might have a chance with this woman. But she's only seen one side of me. She doesn't know what she's getting into.

"Are you sure, Isla? Life isn't always easy for me. You've seen the best of me, but some days are still dark. Sometimes I get frustrated. I get embarrassed, moving around can be slow. It's easy for me here because the entire clubhouse has been adapted to be accessible for me. But it's not like that everywhere. I don't like going out much because a lot of places aren't accessible to me, and sometimes just walking along the pavement is impossible. It's frustrating as hell, and it can be limiting."

She squeezes my hands. "I don't care, Luke. I want to be with you on that journey. I want to ease your frustrations and be there with you." She looks down. "If you want me too, that is."

I hear the vulnerability in her voice. She's put herself out there. She's offering me everything I ever wanted. I tilt her chin up so she's looking at me.

"As long as you're sure Isla, because if we're doing this, then I'm all in. I may have half a body, but I've got a full heart. And I will love you and Cody like he's my own. Ever since you came here three weeks ago, you're all I've wanted.

"I've learned to live with my disability and I've found a life I love here, but for the first time in a long time I doubted myself. I doubted if I was enough."

She shakes her head. "You stupid man. You're more than enough, Luke. You're everything to me."

I pull her onto my chair and wrap one arm around her, pulling her close.

"I love you, Isla, and I'll love and protect you for as long as you want me around. I've loved you since the moment you walked into the clubhouse. I'll fight for you, I'll stay strong for you, and what I lack in body, I'll make up for in devotion. You're my everything."

She puts her hands around my neck and I kiss her slowly and soft, letting every emotion bubble up out of my chest and into the kiss. My hand slides up her back, and holding her in my arms feels so fucking good.

With my other hand I wheel over to the bed, and Isla

jerks back as I bump into the bedpost. "Sorry, you're distracting me."

She smiles and climbs off my lap, and I grab her hand before she can go anywhere. "Is Cody down for the night?"

She glances at the baby monitor where the screen shows him peacefully sleeping in the basinet. "He shouldn't wake for a few hours at least."

I brush my thumb over the pulse of her wrist, feeling it beat against my callused skin. "Stay with me."

Her gaze meets mine, and I bring her hand to my lips and kiss the tender skin of her wrist. She gasps as I graze my lips over the underside of her wrist, her pulse throbbing against my lips.

"I want to show you what you mean to me."

Isla smiles shyly. "I'd like that."

She looks between me and the bed, and I see the question in her eyes. My instinct is to ask her to turn away while I use the transfer board to get myself onto the bed. But if I'm going to be her man, she has to see all of me. I have to show her my vulnerable side, and that's scary as hell.

I pull out the plastic green transfer board I keep by the bed and position it next to my chair. Isla tilts her head, looking curious, and suddenly I don't want her to see this.

"Turn around."

Isla furrows her brows at me. "Why?"

"I don't want you to see this."

She puts her hand on her hips. "Luke, if you think I'm

going to be scared off by seeing you use a transfer board to get into bed, then you're stupider than I thought."

I raise my eyebrows in surprise. "How do you know what a transfer board is?"

"You're not the only one who knows how to use Google."

She reaches for the board and places it on the bed, near the pillow. "May I?" she asks, and I nod before she slides the other end under my body.

"You learned how to do this?" My voice chokes on the emotion welling up inside me. While I've been Googling how to look after a newborn, Isla's been searching for how to look after me.

"I might have watched a couple of videos." She smiles. "Did I do it right?"

I nod, not trusting myself to speak.

I place my hands on the board and pull myself onto the bed. It's less embarrassing than I thought it would be. And Isla slides the board back in its place beside the bed then climbs onto the bed like it's no big deal.

My heart swells for this woman, for her acceptance of me.

"I love you, Isla." I pull her down to the mattress, and we lie side by side. Tendrils of hair escape from her messy bun and tickle my nose. I sweep them away and cup her cheek in my hand.

"I swear I'll do all I can to protect you, to love you and to give you and Cody the best life I can."

I don't make oaths lightly, but this is one is easy to make.

I run my hand over her cheek, and she leans into it. "And the other babies we're going to have," she says.

My eyes widen, and I jolt onto my elbows in shock. "You want more babies?"

Before I got blown up in Afghanistan, I was too young to think about having a family. And after the accident, I didn't think I'd ever have one. Now, the thought of having kids with Isla loosens something deep inside, a longing I never knew I had.

"As long as it's what you want," she adds quickly.

I stroke her cheek. "Oh honey…" The words choke in my throat. I never thought I'd be a father. "I'll give you more babies if that's what you want. Let me be a father to Cody, and I'll show you what a father I can be."

Tears shine in her eyes, and I wipe them away with my thumb. "I already know you'll make a great dad."

Her words ease my last doubts. This is really happening. I've got my woman, and we have a future together. Pure happiness shoots through my veins, and a huge grin spreads over my face.

"We better get some practice in."

She giggles, and I kiss her through the smile and through the tears. Isla sighs into my mouth, and I kiss her harder. My hand snakes into her hair and I loosen the top knot, letting her hair cascade over her shoulders.

"You're beautiful."

She raises an eyebrow. "In a milk-stained top and hair I haven't washed in four days?"

I look down at her top critically. It hugs her breasts in

the most delicious way. "You're right. This top needs to come off."

My fingers tremble as I undo the top button of her checkered shirt. It's been a long time since I undressed a woman and never one who I loved the way I love Isla.

Slowly I unravel her, button by button until the shirt falls open. Isla's hand jolts up to cover her maternity bra.

"I don't have any other bras that fit at the moment." She bites her bottom lip, looking embarrassed. But I couldn't care less about the plain practical bra.

I pry her fingers gently away. "We better get this off too."

She giggles, and I reach around behind her to undo the clasp. I'm out of practice and my fingers fumble. "I feel like a fucking virgin. It's been so long."

Isla smiles. "I like that. I'd be worried if you could undo a maternity bra one handed."

She undoes the clasp, and the straps go loose on her shoulders. I slide the bra down her shoulders and suck in my breath when it falls off, revealing her heavy breasts.

My dick jerks in my pants, and I almost lose it. "Fuck, Isla, you're fucking gorgeous."

I cup her left breast and press my lips to the skin. My research tells me she'll be sensitive so I bypass the nipples, caressing every other part of her instead.

Her hands run down my chest, and she tugs at the bottom of my t-shirt. I help her shrug it off and discard it on the floor next to her clothes.

Her hands trail over my body, and my muscles flex under her touch. Her fingertips brush against my hard chest, making my skin heat. Then she leans forward to kiss my chest.

Every press of her lips has jolts of heat coursing through my body. My body's on fire, and every flame leads to my dick. I'm so hard it's painful.

I long to be inside her, but I'm not sure how the logistics are going to work. I'm not sure if I can balance or what positions are best for a double amputee. So I go on instinct, leaning into her and pressing our bodies together, loving how it feels good and how her little whimpers tell me it's good for her.

Her hand glides lower down my chest, and I suck in a nervous breath when she gets to my lower torso. "Can I touch you down there?"

I know what she's asking. No one touches what remains of my legs except my physical therapist. But if I'm going to let Isla in, I need to let her in all the way.

"Yes." My voice is little more than a croak. "If you want to."

Her hand glides over my bulge and to the top of my left thigh. It's been so long since anyone touched me there that the sensation makes my phantom leg jerk. Isla pauses and turns her questioning gaze to me, asking silently if this is still okay.

I hold my breath and nod. This is more intimate that I ever imagined, and it scares the shit out of me. What if she's turned off by what she finds? I fight the urge to push her away and instead unbutton my jeans.

"Take your pants off," I instruct her. If I'm going to expose all of me, then I want both of us naked.

I wriggle out of my jeans, then take a deep breath and pull down my briefs. Our clothes are discarded on the floor. And then we're both naked. Since the accident, I haven't been naked in front of anyone who wasn't a medical professional. I'm thankful for the dim light.

I'm breathing hard and terrified she'll be turned off by what she sees. I hold my breath as she traces her fingers up my inner thigh. At the same time her lips press to my right nipple, and the sensation makes me jerk against her. My hardness bumps into her arm, and Isla giggles.

"I guess you like that."

"Honey, I like everything you do to me."

"Then open your eyes."

I didn't realize I had them closed, or that I was holding my breath. When I open them, Isla's watching me, her eyes dark pools of desire.

And it finally hits me. She doesn't care about my missing limbs; she's not turned off by them. She wants my body as much as she wants my heart. If such a thing is possible, I fall for her even more.

"Fuck, I love you, Isla." My voice comes out low and husky, and I slide my arm around her waist and pull her against me.

"I love you too, Luke."

This time when I kiss her it's urgent and hungry. Our bodies slide together, and my hardness presses against her soft belly. She opens her legs, and I pull her thigh over mine as my cock glides between her wetness.

I no longer think about what I'm lacking. All I can

think about is moving my body to please Isla. I watch her expression to figure out what she likes as I glide between her folds.

My hand runs over her hip and her ass as I explore the contours of her body. We move together, lying side my side. But that's not how I want to take my woman. I want to show her I can still take control in the bedroom.

Grabbing her shoulders, I flip Isla onto her back, making her gasp as I roll myself on top of her. Her eyes widen in surprise as I pin her down with my arms.

"Luke…" She moans my name as her hips thrust up to meet mine. Her thighs part for me, and I release her enough to guide myself into her.

We both groan as I sink inside.

Isla feels like heaven and everything good I've been missing. She clamps around me, and I squeeze my eyes shut before I lose control.

"Fuck, Isla, you feel incredible."

I've never been more grateful for getting back to the gym as I prop myself up with my arms, using my strength to rock back and forth, sliding deeper with every thrust.

Isla wraps her legs around my buttocks, wordlessly providing the leverage I need to push deeper. I lean forward to kiss her neck and cheeks and lips and the sensitive place behind her ear that makes her body jerk when I press my lips to it.

I try to take it slow, but I'm unable to hold back the tide of emotion and sensations building inside of me. I give her everything I have as I lose myself in Isla, in the woman I love.

"Luke…" Isla's moans turn to whimpers. Then she tenses under me and comes in a wave of heat and noise that breaks through my last restraints.

The dam bursts and a wave of bliss crashes over me, consuming every last doubt I had. Isla is mine, and I'll make love to her every fucking day for the rest of my life.

I hold her close as I explode into her and she trembles under me, whimpering my name over and over again.

Afterwards we lie side by side talking long into the night.

Around midnight, Isla gets up to feed Cody and I join her, watching her with our son.

Then we go back to bed and make love two more times before Isla falls into a deep sleep. I watch her sleeping with her hair falling over the pillow and her mouth slightly open.

My chest feels like it might burst as I watch her, my woman.

Isla reminded me of what it means to be a man. She made me whole, and I'll spend the rest of my life being the man she needs.

EPILOGUE

LUKE

One Year Later...

*T*he wedding march starts playing, and all heads in the church turn to watch Isla. Her dress bunches at the waist and fans out over her hips, showing off her curves. Tendrils of hair fall in curls over her bare shoulders.

My breath catches, and my stomach flutters with nerves. I still can't believe that this beautiful, amazing woman agreed to marry me. She's looking down and my stomach clenches, wondering if she's having doubts. My missing left limb twitches, and I long to scratch it. I'm wearing my prosthetics today. I wanted to look my wife in the eye when we pledged our lives to each other.

I still prefer my wheelchair but I've been using the

prosthetics more, especially now that Cody's walking. It's easier to chase after the little guy with my prosthetics, although his favorite thing is to take a spin on my wheels.

Isla steps onto the red carpet that runs down the aisle of the church. Her head comes up and her gaze finds mine. She smiles a warm smile that's all for me.

My stomach relaxes and my chest warms. There's a church full of people, but it feels like it's just the two of us.

I grin back at Isla, my soon to be wife, and my heart is full. I'm the luckiest motherfucker alive.

"Mommy." Cody squirms from his place on his Uncle Ryan's knee and reaches a chubby hand out to Isla. Her gaze turns to him, and she gives him a little wave. Cody giggles and that makes the entire congregation laugh.

Isla's brother Ryan turned up soon after we officially got together with his pregnant wife, Julia, and young son in tow. He was unhappy they were detained in Italy and initially was weary of me and my intentions toward his sister. Being part of a motorcycle club, people have pre-conceptions of what we're like. But it didn't take long for him to relax, especially when he saw how devoted I am to Isla and Cody. And when Isla told him the story of how I saw off Ian, he slapped me on the back and bought me a beer. We've become good friends and Isla and Ryan video chat regularly, and Cody loves seeing his cousins online.

Isla even convinced me to visit them. I was nervous leaving Wild Heart Mountain and the place that's become my entire life. But with her help and patience we navigated the long drive, finding the rest stops that had accessible facilities and passing those that didn't.

We stayed at a motel close to her brother's place. He had hastily put in a ramp to the front door and has plans to make the rest of their house accessible for the next time we visit. I was touched by the acceptance from Isla's family.

Her mother took a while to come around, still thinking Isla should go back to Ian. But when Ian started posting nasty lies about Isla on social media, she finally accepted he wasn't the golden boy she thought he was. Her best friend and Ian's mother finally admitted he had issues, and they've found him a good therapist.

I adapted the designs for my cabin, and the guys helped me build it. Our cabin in the woods is all on one level. There are ramps where needed, and the rooms are wide enough to turn my chair in without hitting the furniture. Shelving and cupboards are down low where I can reach them, and every bathroom is set up for my ease of use.

I have a home gym and four bedrooms, plenty of space when Ryan and Julia come to visit with the kids, and room for our family to grow.

We've decided to take it slow on that front. I'm longing to put a baby in Isla's belly, but we have to be realistic about what I can handle. Chasing one toddler around the house is fine, but two might be too much, especially while we're finishing up the cabin. We'll wait a bit longer before trying for another baby. Although as I look at Isla coming down the aisle, radiant in her wedding dress, I wonder if I'll be able to wait that long.

She reaches the front of the church, and her father kisses her on the cheek before she steps into place next to me.

I take her hands and run my thumbs over her soft skin.

Specs is officiating for us, and he clears his throat. His gaze darts to someone in the crowd, and I bet it's that shy bookworm friend of Isabella's he's been ogling for years. The problem is they're both too shy to do anything about it.

But that's not my concern. I have my woman, and I'm ready to make her my wife.

Specs reads the ceremony, but I hardly hear him. I race through my vows, eager to get to the part where I kiss my bride.

Isla licks her lips and my gaze darts to them, full and pink with make-up. Then Specs declares us husband and wife.

I take Isla in my arms and our lips crash together; it's supposed to be a gentle kiss to seal the deal, but I haven't seen her in two days because of wedding prep, and as soon as my lips meet hers, hunger for my wife consumes me.

We kiss long and hard until catcalls from the congregation have us pulling apart. I'm panting hard, and I can't wait to get my wife alone to consummate this marriage.

"Daddy." Cody breaks free and toddles on his unsteady legs towards us. "Daddy." He reaches out his hands to me and I lift him up, making him giggle.

I never thought I'd be blessed with my own family. But here I am. My MC brothers, Isla and Cody. I'm the luckiest man alive.

* * *

GET YOUR FREE BOOKS

Sign up to the Sadie King mailing list and get access to all the bonus content including bonus scenes and five FREE steamy short romances!

You'll be the first to hear about new releases, exclusive offers, bonus content and all my news. You can even email me back. I love chatting with my readers!

To claim your free books visit:
authorsadieking.com/bonus-scenes

If you're already a subscriber check your last email for the link that will take you straight to the bonus content.

BOOKS & SERIES BY SADIE KING

Wild Heart Mountain

Military Heroes

Kobe brings together a group of military veterans who live on the side of Wild Heart Mountain. Can these wounded warriors find love or do their scars cut too deep?

Wild Riders MC

This group of ex-military bikers fall hard and fall fast when they encounter the curvy women who heal their hearts.

Mountain Heroes

Steamy stories featuring the men and women from Wild Heart Mountain's Search and Rescue and Fire service.

Temptation

A damaged hero and a lost virgin in an explosive instalove retelling of the Hansel and Gretel story set in the woods of Wild Heart Mountain.

A Runaway Bride for Christmas

A snowstorm keeps this runaway bride trapped in the cabin of the mountain's biggest grump.

Sunset Coast

Underground Crows MC

Short and steamy MC romance stories of obsessed men and curvy girls.

Sunset Security

A security firm run by ex-military men who become obsessed with their curvy girls.

Men of the Sea

Super short and steamy tales from Temptation Bay of bad boys and curvy girls.

Love and Obsession

A bad boy trilogy featuring a thief, a henchman and an ex-military hitman who finds redemption with his curvy girl.

Filthy Rich Love

The billionaires of the Sunset Coast. These alpha men fall hard and fall fast for the younger curvy women who crash into their world.

Maple Springs

Small Town Sisters

Five curvy sister's inherit a dog hotel. But can they find love? Short and steamy instalove romance!

Candy's Café

A small-town cafe that's all heart. Meet the sister's who run it and the customer's who keep coming back.

All the Single Dads

These single dad hotties are fiercely protective and will do anything for the ones they love.

Men of Maple Mountain

These men are OTT possessive and will stop at nothing to claim the curvy innocent women they become obsessed with.

The Carter Family

Blue collar men find love with curvy girls in these quick read instalove romances.

Curvy Girls Can

Short, sweet and steamy instalove stories about sassy curvy women and the men who love them.

For a full list of Sadie King's books check out her website

www.authorsadieking.com

ABOUT THE AUTHOR

Sadie King is a USA Today Best Selling Author of contemporary romance novellas.

She lives in New Zealand with her ex-military husband and raucous young son.

When she's not writing she loves catching waves with her son, running along the beach, and drinking good wine with a book in hand.

Keep in touch when you sign up for her newsletter. You'll snag yourself a free short romance and access to all the bonus content!

authorsadieking.com/bonus-scenes

Printed in Great Britain
by Amazon